The Adventures of
Titch & Mitch

The Adventures of
Titch & Mitch

Book 4
The Magic Boots

Garth Edwards
Illustrated by Max Stasyuk

INSIDE
POCKET

Published in Great Britain by Inside Pocket Publishing Limited

First published in Great Britain in 2010

Text © Garth Edwards, 2009

The right of Garth Edwards to be identified as the author of this work
has been asserted in accordance with the Copyright, Designs and Patents
Act 1988.

Illustrations © Inside Pocket Publishing Limited

Titch and Mitch is a registered trade mark of Inside Pocket Publishing
Limited

A CIP catalogue record for this book is available from the British Library

ISBN 978-0-9562315-3-6

Inside Pocket Publishing Limited Reg. No. 06580097

Printed and bound in Great Britain by CPI Bookmarque Ltd, Croydon

www.insidepocket.co.uk

For N & J

Contents

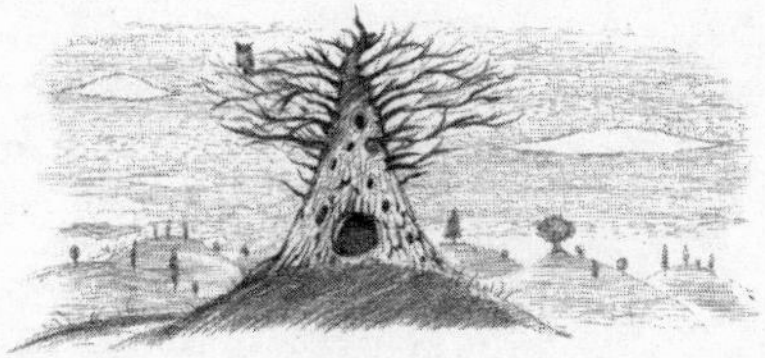

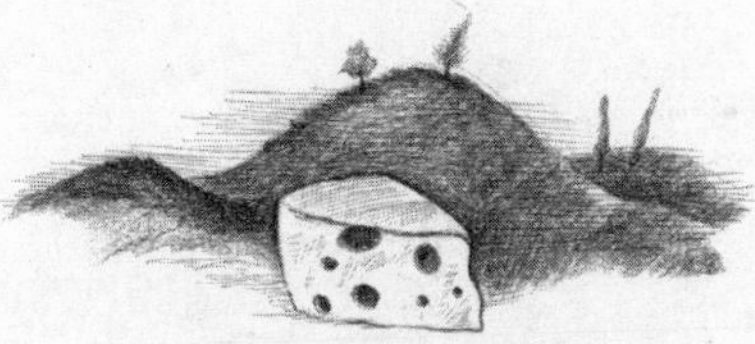

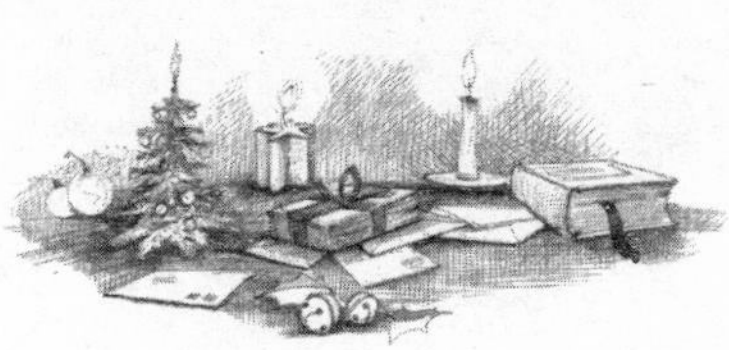

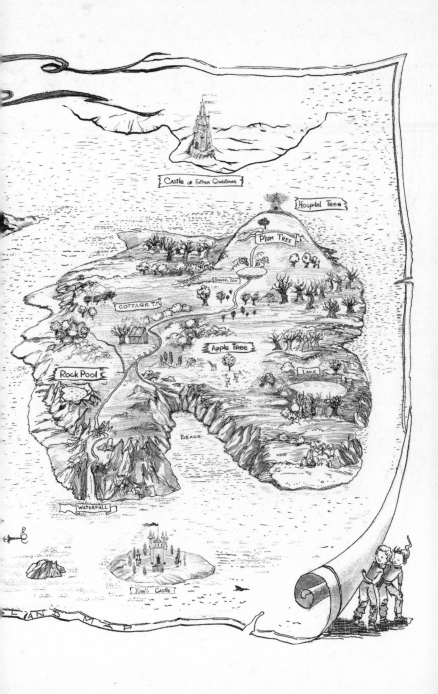

1

The Magic Boots

A LONG TIME AGO, SOMEWHERE NOT VERY
far away from where Titch and Mitch live on their
island, a mighty wizard once made a pair of magic
boots. Whenever he wore these strange and unusual
boots, he was able to run very fast and jump very
high.

For many years, the only person who used them
was the wizard himself. He would stride about the
countryside, visiting anywhere he wanted, running
and jumping and never getting tired. They really
were wonderful boots and quite the envy of anyone
who saw them in action. And what is more, despite
their frequent use, they never wore out or seemed to

tire of jumping and springing and bouncing.

The wizard himself lived in a tower on the outskirts of a small village. When he became very old, he went into the village and said to the Mayor,

'One day I will die and I want you to sell the tower where I live and use the money to help all the people in the village. You must sell the tower to people who will look after it, and you must give my boots to whomsoever they fit. I will leave the boots in the room at the top of the tower so that anybody can try them on. Only when the boots have gone to a good home can you sell the tower, but I must warn you, the boots will only leave the tower with somebody they like.'

Misty was telling the

story of the magic boots to a captivated
audience of Titch, Mitch, Wiffen and
Perry. They were all sitting around a
barbeque in the garden of the little
cottage where Wiffen and Perry
lived. The two pixies often visited
their friends Wiffen, the intelligent
turkey, and Perry, the Old English
sheepdog. This time, they had been
joined by their friend Misty, a
beautiful fairy with white, gossamer
wings who lived nearby in the
valley of fairies.

As they listened, enraptured,
she carried on with her mysterious
story.

"When the old wizard died,
some years ago, the tower was put
up for sale and the Mayor was quite
confident that the

boots would soon find a good home. He was, in fact, the first person to try them on, and he was very disappointed to find they didn't fit. But it was very strange, because, you see, although he could get his feet into the boots, and they felt quite snug and comfortable, the boots themselves refused to move."

"They didn't move?" puzzled Titch.

"It's true!" she said, eyes sparkling in the warm firelight. "They

wouldn't even lift themselves off the ground, so the Mayor had to find somebody else to take them away."

"Who did they fit?" asked Mitch.

"Well, that's the problem," continued Misty. "The boots didn't fit anybody at all. They have been sitting in the top room of that tower for more than two years now. Everybody for miles around has tried them on. Even the big, fat King of the Castle made the long journey to see if they would fit him, but the boots wouldn't budge an inch. The thing is," she said, leaning in close, "if the boots don't like the wearer, they simply fasten themselves to the ground so hard that nobody can

lift them, no matter how
strong they are."

Titch, Mitch,
Wiffen and Perry all
gasped at the very
thought of a pair of
boots with a mind of
their own.

"How extraordinary,"
said Wiffen. "What a
curious tale."

Misty continued,
"Sometimes, they do
change their shape a little to fit the foot
that goes into them, and it looks as if they are
thinking about the person. But then they suddenly
change their minds completely and go back to their
original shape, which can be jolly painful if you're the
one with your foot stuck inside. Honestly," she said,
sitting back and folding one leg over another, "there
have been gnomes, goblins, pixies, elves, trolls,
fairies; every two-legged creature you can think of,
but the boots haven't liked any of them, not a single
one. It's quite remarkable."

There was a moment's silence as everyone
stopped to think about the strange boots and their

odd behaviour. It was Wiffen who broke the silence at last.

"So the boots are still there, waiting to find a new owner," he observed thoughtfully. Then, turning to Titch and Mitch in a state of obvious excitement, he said, "You pixies are very nice creatures; perhaps you should try them on for size."

"That's exactly what I thought," said Misty. "It's very important for the fairies, because we want to buy the tower. We need a resting place outside the valley, and the tower is ideal for travelling fairies to fly in at the top window. Unfortunately, we can't buy it until the boots are gone, which is why I'm telling you the story. I would like Titch and Mitch to try on the boots. I'm sure they will like you."

"It sounds exciting," said Mitch, very confident that the boots would choose him. Overall, he thought to himself, he was the nicer of the two of them, and the boots were bound to fit him perfectly.

"Of course," added Titch, thinking very much the same thing. "We must try on the boots!" he exclaimed.

"I wouldn't miss this for the world," said Wiffen, flapping his wings excitedly. "I wonder which of you the boots will like." Then, as an afterthought, he added, "Perhaps you can both share the boots. What do you think, Perry?"

The sheepdog shook his shaggy head and, after a few moments thought, replied, very diplomatically, "I think you are very nice pixies and the boots will be pleased to fit both of you. Perhaps we should all go together."

"That's settled then," said Misty. "We can go first thing in the morning."

Bright and early the very next morning, Wiffen, in a state of high excitement, climbed briskly onto Perry's back and, digging his claws deep into the sheepdog's fur, said, "Come on Perry, let's go and find this tower!"

With the two pixies hovering on their magic bicycle and Misty flying gently alongside, the little expedition set off in search of the Wizard's tower and his magic boots.

Around midday, they arrived at a little village on the edge of a very big wood. On the far side of the village, reaching high up into the clouds, they saw the wizard's tower. Titch and Mitch, and even Wiffen, gasped at the sight. It was far bigger and much more imposing than any of them had at first thought.

"We must go and see the Mayor first," said Misty. "He has the key to the tower and he always likes to be present when anyone tries on the boots."

They landed in front of a smart, half-timbered house in the middle of the village.

After they knocked, the door was opened by an old lady with white hair bound in a red ribbon. When she spotted Misty, she beamed and said, "Ahh, you have brought the very nice pixies to try on the boots, have you? The

Mayor is at the tower right now. Some very nice trolls came along and insisted that they try on the boots."

"Nice trolls," said Wiffen, snorting with disgust. "There is no such thing as a nice troll."

"Oh, these trolls are very friendly," the old lady insisted. "They come almost every week without fail."

"I'd call that very silly," said Wiffen, speaking down the length of his beak.

"I'd call it unlucky," added Perry. "They're obviously trying very hard to get the boots."

Taking their leave, the friends made their way out of the village and soon came to the tall tower. Once again they found themselves astounded by the sight that greeted them. Though it was very tall and very old, it was also very narrow, little more than the width of a spiral staircase. At various points up the sides there were small windows and it was topped by a pointed roof covered in red slates. On one side there jutted out a small wooden balcony that looked as though it had been clipped onto the side as an afterthought.

Narrowing his eyes, Wiffen looked up the full length of the tower and tutted quietly to himself, though loud enough for the others to hear quite clearly.

"It looks very crooked," he said at last, squinting upwards. "I'm not so sure about this at all."

"It will be super for the fairies," said Misty. "We can fly straight into that room at the top and it'll be a perfect place to stop off for a rest. Oh, I do hope the boots like one of you."

As they stood looking up at the tower, the Mayor came out of the little door at the bottom. He was breathing heavily and wiping his brow with a dirty, grey rag. He was a small man, round and quite sturdy, with a shiny, bald head and a large red nose. He was followed out of the tower by two huge trolls who both had long, hairy arms and grim, scowling faces.

"Well, I'm sorry you've wasted your time once again," said the Mayor, with barely concealed irritation. "See you next week."

The trolls glared at the pixies as they passed, and one of them said, "If the boots don't like delicious trolls like us, they certainly won't like horrid little pixies like you two."

Then, with a snigger, he added, "Why don't you come and work for us. There's a job down the mines in Sugar Loaf Wood."

The two pixies shrank back, and Mitch could be seen to shiver from head to foot, but Wiffen went bright red with rage and glared at the trolls with his

beady, little eyes.

"Perry," he growled, staring each one right in the eye. "Show me how fast those trolls can run."

With a sudden bound, Perry leapt forward and stood stiff legged in front of the trolls. He growled deeply and fiercely then moved slowly forward growling and snarling. The trolls jumped backwards in alarm and, turning quickly, they ran away towards the village and soon disappeared around a corner.

Once they had gone, Titch explained to the

Mayor why Mitch in
particular was not very keen
on trolls. "They have these
mines in Sugar Loaf Wood,"
he started to say.

"I know," said the Mayor.
"I've heard about the mines. No
wonder the boots reject them. But still
they come, week after week. What
can I do?"

With a heavy sigh, he wiped once
again at the beads of sweat forming
on his brow and sat down on a small
wooden chair to catch his breath.

"You know, some people get quite
cross when the boots don't like
them, and then they shout at me
as if it was my fault, but it's not.
I'm just the keyholder. I'd love
them to fit somebody. I'd love
to get rid of the boots and
never see another troll for as
long as I live. Do you know
how many stairs there are
in that tower? Can you
guess how many times I've

climbed them? And all for nothing! I've got other work to do, you know? I'm the Mayor!"

Titch and Mitch nodded, sympathetic to the poor fellow's plight.

"Anyway," the Mayor said at last. "What can I do for you?"

"Well," said Titch slowly, not wishing to scare the fellow with the thought of another climb up the tower so soon, but, before he could continue, Mitch butted in.

"We'd like to see the boots, please," he said, eagerly.

"Oh…" sighed the Mayor, and looked like he might slide off his chair and slump to the ground. However, with an effort, he recovered himself and, getting to his feet, said to them brightly, "Come on then, let's climb the stairs. It's only four thousand, six hundred and ninety two steps. Not so many really, once you get used to them." So saying, he led them on their way.

It was a long climb, and quite exhausting for everyone, except the Mayor himself, who really did seem quite used to the climb after all. Finally, the party arrived at the room at the top of the tower. It was a small room and perfectly circular. On the far side, opposite the door where they came in, was another leading to the balcony they had seen from the ground. The door was open slightly and cool air wafted in from outside, which they all found quite welcoming after the hot, sweaty climb.

In the middle of the room, sitting on the rough wooden floor, was a pair of very ordinary looking boots. They were brown with round, shiny toes at the front and a solid sole underneath. They had leather laces, which enabled the boots to be strapped up over the ankles but overall there was nothing unusual about them.

The Mayor stood in front of them and, with an air of ceremony, introduced the two pixies. "My dear boots," he said. "Allow me to introduce to you two very nice pixies. I have heard from Misty the fairy that they do good works all over the place and they already have a magic bicycle, so you would have some magic company if you go with one of them. Please choose either Titch or Mitch," then he added hopefully, "or both of them, if you so wish."

There was no response from the boots. They didn't move, speak or waggle anything to show that they understood what the Mayor was saying. With a nod from his brother, Titch stepped forward, removed his shoes, took a deep breath and approached the boots. He took the left one in both hands and lifted

it off the ground. There was a
sharp intake of breath from
the Mayor, who whispered
excitedly to the others,
"That's good. Not
many creatures can
get them off the
floor at all. They
must like Titch
at least a bit."

Slipping his
foot into the left
boot and standing upright, Titch beamed happily at
his friends and said, "That's a good fit."

They all gasped when he lifted his foot off the
ground and the left boot came with it. The Mayor
clapped his hands with delight, but held his breath as
Titch slipped his other foot into the right boot.
Standing up with both feet in the boots, Titch smiled
happily. "I've got magic boots," he whispered to
everyone.

The Mayor said, "You must walk round the room
to make sure they like you."

Boldly, and with a broad smile, Titch took a step
forward. But, alas, only the left boot moved. The
right boot stayed firmly and resolutely on the ground.

No matter how hard Titch tried, the right boot simply would not budge.

He looked at his friends, his little face crumpled, his hand went to his mouth, tears eased their way out of his eyes and he said in a strained voice, "The right boot, it won't move, it doesn't like me."

"I'm so sorry," said the Mayor, shaking his head sadly.

Bending down, Titch unlaced the boots, stepped out of them and walked to his friends looking very sad indeed. "Your turn," he mumbled to Mitch as he stood next to him.

Mitch was very surprised. He had been quite sure that the boots would like Titch. He was now very nervous and approached the boots slowly.

This time, Mitch tried the right boot on first. He was delighted to find it fitted him perfectly and easily lifted off the ground. He smiled happily and reached down to try on the left boot that had liked Titch. It fitted him nicely as well and, taking a deep breath, he lifted his left foot off the ground. Or rather, he tried to lift it off the ground, but once again the boot refused to move.

"I don't believe it," cried the Mayor. "The left foot likes Titch and the right foot likes Mitch. What can we do?"

"This is most unexpected and very upsetting," said Misty with a note of irritation in her voice. "Perhaps if Titch were to wear the left boot, and Mitch could put on the right boot, they could both hop out of the room and take the boots home. When the boots get to know them they will like them better and they can all live happily ever after."

The Mayor shrugged. "It's worth a try," he said glumly.

So, with a great deal of trepidation, the two pixies did exactly as Misty suggested. Unfortunately, this plan didn't work either, because neither boot would let itself be moved.

"I'm so sorry boys," said the Mayor at last. "It's the nearest we've been to finding a home for the boots, but it seems that unless they both like one of you, there's nothing we can do."

Sadly, the pixies took off the boots and left them standing in the middle of the room exactly as they had found them.

"Come on," said the Mayor with a very glum

expression. "Let's go down again. Maybe some other day…" And he turned slowly towards the door.

"Wait a minute," said Wiffen quite unexpectedly. "I have an idea. I would like to try the boots on myself."

"You," said the Mayor, quite taken aback at such a curious suggestion. "But you're a turkey!"

"So?" replied Wiffen, ominously. "What has being a turkey got to do with it?"

"Turkey's don't wear boots!" said the Mayor, turning once again to go, and adding, before Wiffen had time to reply, "It would be a waste of time. And as I've already told you, I'm a very busy man."

"I appreciate you being a busy man, Mr Mayor," said Wiffen, growing increasingly angry.

"And you're only a turkey!" snapped the Mayor, waving his hand in the air dismissively.

"Only a turkey!" snarled Wiffen with a deep growl that stopped the Mayor in his tracks. "I'll have you know that I am the most intelligent turkey in the whole world. The boots can change shape, and if they want to fit a turkey, then fit a turkey they will!"

The Mayor stood still, sighed in exasperation and, leaning back against the wall, said, "Oh, go on then. What harm can it do? But be quick about it."

However, Wiffen wasn't to be rushed and turning

back to Titch and Mitch said, "I need to ask you a few questions."

"OK," they nodded. "Ask away."

"First, would you be cruel to your magic bicycle?"

"No," they replied, shocked at such an odd suggestion.

"Would you leave it out in the rain?"

"Certainly not," they said.

"Would you leave it dirty?"

"No."

"Would you drop it on the ground?"

"No."

"Would you kick it out of your way?"

"Of course not," they replied together.

"In which case, I think I know what is worrying the boots."

Leaving the others wondering, Wiffen approached the boots. He stood with his legs apart, his wings drooping slightly and, leaning forward, he looked down at the boots and said in the most agreeable voice he could muster, "Good afternoon boots. My name is Wiffen and I would like, if I may, to try you on."

The others all looked at each other, wondering what on earth Wiffen was up to.

"If you boots should find that you like me as much as I believe I like you, and should you then accept me as your new wearer, then I assure you that you will be well looked after at all times. I promise that you will live in my house and be nice and warm. You won't ever be locked in a cupboard or kept in the dark. If you get wet, I will dry you off quickly and if you get muddy, I will clean you as soon as we get home. I also promise to polish you every day, even if you are not dirty."

There was no response. The two boots sat on the

floor motionless, just as they had been when everyone had entered the room. The Mayor gave a sigh and looked up at the ceiling. But, as he looked down again, he noticed something very odd. The others noticed it too.

Slowly, and without a sound, the boots turned towards each other in a smooth gliding motion and paused for a second, as if consulting. Then, again smoothly and silently, they turned back to face Wiffen, the laces unravelled, the tops of the boots spread themselves out and the tongues flopped forward.

Without hesitation, Wiffen stepped forward and raised his left claw. It slid nicely into the left boot. Then he raised his right claw and slid it into the other boot. As the friends watched with amazement, the two boots gradually changed shape to fit perfectly the turkey's hooked feet and sharp claws. Finally, the laces straightened themselves out and tied themselves together in a neat bow.

"Oh, my goodness," exclaimed the Mayor, his face changing in colour from red to white. Clapping his hands together, he said, "You are indeed the most intelligent turkey in the world! Why did nobody else work out that boots have likes and dislikes, just like everybody else?"

Wiffen looked around him and smirked happily.

"You see?" he said proudly. "All they needed was a little reassurance."

He lifted one boot in the air and then the other. In a moment he was walking round the room,

shaking his wattle, gobbling happily and preening all his feathers. Actually, it was more of a sliding motion that the boots preferred to use, so it seemed to his friends that Wiffen simply glided round the room effortlessly.

"You can tell everyone the boots are gone now," Wiffen said to the startled Mayor, and added graciously, "You can get back to your busy work."

"And the fairies can now have the tower," said Misty in delight, "We've been waiting a long time."

They all walked down the steps of the tower and as soon as they got outside, Wiffen and his magic boots ran around in circles and jumped high in the air. "This is marvellous!" he shouted, "Wonderful!" And, turning to Perry, he added. "I won't have to hang on to your fur now when we go travelling."

"Oh good," replied Perry. "You are too heavy for me anyway."

As it was starting to get dark, they all decided it was time to go home and so they said goodbye to the Mayor who joyfully handed the keys of the tower to Misty.

Titch and Mitch jumped on their magic bicycle and called out the magic words, "Up, up and away." Immediately the bicycle hovered into the air and the friends started on their journey home. Perry ran alongside Wiffen, who was bounding along so fast that the poor dog found it difficult to follow the excited turkey.

"Come on Perry, keep up," called out Wiffen. "I can go faster than this you know."

They came to a point where their path crossed a river. Perry slowed down, but Wiffen was going so fast

he couldn't stop and ran blindly towards the water's edge.

"Ahh," he screamed as he stepped off the bank. "Help me!"

With his wings flapping frantically and his little legs racing along, he dived into the river, splashing about wildly, and disappeared under the water. Then, just as the others thought he was about to drown, he suddenly reappeared and, to the amazement of everybody, carried on running on top of the water.

Titch and Mitch landed at the side of the river and stood next to Perry, who was so out of breath he just stood there panting. They watched Wiffen running around in circles on the surface of the river and calling out to them, "Look at me, look at me, I'm running on water!"

Eventually, the excited turkey ran off the water and came to rest next to them. "What wonderful boots," he gasped. "Quite extraordinary!"

Turning to Titch and Mitch, he said, "You know what this means, don't you?"

The pixies looked a bit puzzled and Mitch said, "What does it mean?"

"If I can walk on water, it means I can come over to your island whenever I want. That'll be nice won't it?"

Titch and Mitch looked at each other and said together, "Oh yes! That would be very nice indeed!"

2

The Lion

WIFFEN WAS BEING A PERFECT HOST AND
pouring out a glass of lemonade for his pixie friends,
Titch and Mitch, when the door of his cottage burst
open. Perry, the Old English sheepdog who lived with
Wiffen, raced in and, slamming the door behind him,
stood panting heavily, unable to speak.

"What is it?" demanded Wiffen, who considered
himself to be the most intelligent turkey in the world
and could be very impatient when interrupted. "Why
are you rushing around? You don't normally run
anywhere if you don't have to!"

Perry jumped up to the back window and looked
outside. He raised a paw and pointed to the nearby

woods. "A lion," he gasped through urgent breaths. "A huge, fierce lion roaming the woods!"

"Nonsense!" said Wiffen. "There are no lions in our woods. It was probably a horse or something with a long, hairy mane."

Nevertheless, Titch and Mitch scrambled to the window and joined Perry, still staring towards the nearby trees.

"How far away is it?" said Titch, excitedly.

"How big is it?" shouted Mitch.

"There are no lions in our woods!" screeched Wiffen, flapping his wings angrily.

Before Perry could answer, Budgie the yellow

seagull swooped down and landed on the window ledge. She was a good friend of Wiffen and often dropped in unexpectedly.

"I say you lot, I've just seen a monster lion in the woods and it's coming your way. You'd better hide, it looks hungry to me." Budgie looked over her shoulder and squawked loudly. "There it is! I'm off." With a quick jump into the air, Budgie flew straight up to the top of the house and perched on the chimney.

The seagull was right! As they watched, a lion

had left the shelter of the woods and was strolling slowly towards the cottage. When it reached the front gate, it yawned, swished its tail and stared hard at the cottage with bright yellow eyes.

There were two pairs of eyes peeping over the window ledge and staring back at the lion. They belonged to Titch and Mitch who wanted to join Wiffen and Perry hiding under the table, but were too terrified to move.

The lion came nearer and nearer until the pixies could see large bushy eyebrows, little black specks in the yellow eyes, and scars around the great mouth. When the lion pushed its shaggy head in through the window, Titch and Mitch both leaped backwards together and landed in a heap on the floor.

"Ahh, pixies," rumbled the lion, looking straight at them. "Do you live here?"

"N-N-N-No," stammered Mitch, and pointing towards the table said, "they live here, and I'm sure you are welcome to a drink of lemonade, but I'm afraid that my brother and I must be going. We are already late for something." The two pixies backed towards the front door clutching each other for support.

"How very kind of you. A drink would be nice if you have a bowl big enough," the lion rumbled again.

"Who are you and what do you want?" Wiffen called out from under the table in a very strained voice.

"My name is Edgar and if you haven't noticed I'm a lion. I work at the circus in town and I'm looking for my friend Shrimp, the monkey."

Wiffen peeped out from under the table. "Are you hungry and looking for something to eat?"

"Not at all!" replied the lion indignantly. "And even if I were, I wouldn't eat a pixie, or a dog or..." Edgar hesitated before adding, "...or a turkey, no matter how plump and tasty it looked. But I am a little thirsty."

Wiffen retreated back under the table and nudged Perry with his wing. "Perry," he said urgently. "Fetch your bowl and give Edgar a drink."

"Why me?" said Perry, still unwilling to get too close to the lion.

"Because he's your lion, you saw him first!" snapped Wiffen. "Now get a move on."

Obediently, Perry sidled out from under the table and dragged his bowl over towards the window. Titch poured out some lemonade for the lion and placed the bowl on the sill. Edgar drank it all. He then licked his lips and said, "That was very tasty lemonade, thank you. Now, have any of you seen a little tree monkey anywhere? He's about the same size as you pixies, but has a long tail and leaps about very quickly."

Titch, Mitch, Wiffen and Perry all tried to remember if they had seen a monkey anywhere, when they were startled by a voice shouting down the chimney.

"Are you all right down there? The lion's got his head stuck in through your window!" It was Budgie, still perched on the roof. "I hope he isn't eating you."

"We're fine, thank you Budgie," Titch shouted back up the chimney. "We're just having a little chat."

Wiffen ventured out from under the table, full of curiosity. "How did you escape from the circus? And what brought you to our woods?" he said.

Edgar rumbled on. "It's a travelling circus and we go anywhere and everywhere. Occasionally, however, I like to take a little stroll on my own, reconnect with nature, that sort of thing."

"But how do you get out?" asked Wiffen, hopping up onto a chair near the window.

"My cage has an old, broken lock," the lion explained. "I can undo it anytime I want. But, I have to be careful. If anybody saw me, the lock would get mended and that would be the end of my adventures. That's why I normally wander at night; there's much less chance of being seen."

"What do you do in the circus?" asked Mitch.

"Silly things really, nothing difficult. I jump through a hoop and stand on a box, but mostly I roar to frighten the children. For some strange reason children like to be frightened."

"Are there other lions?" asked Mitch.

"Oh yes, there's my friend Horace. We share a

cage together but he's an old lion and doesn't want to come out with me when I go wandering. Then, there are the tigers. I don't like them much; they scratch you know. Quite a lot actually, look at the scars on my mouth. Whenever I walk past them they lash out at me for no reason, so I keep away from them. If you see a tiger wandering in the woods, take my advice and stay away from it."

"Oh, we will! But why don't they like you?" asked Wiffen.

"They don't like anybody. Bad tempered and nasty creatures they are. I suppose they're not really happy being in the circus, but I've rather grown used to it. I'm sure that's what annoys them."

"And who is Shrimp?" Mitch had to ask because he had never seen a monkey and was very curious.

"A little rascal, that's what he is. He lives in a cage opposite mine and is always chattering away. Just as I was popping out last night, I stopped for a quick chat with his mother and Shrimp squeezed through the bars at the top of his cage and jumped down on to my back. His mother called him back to the cage but he refused, so she made him promise to stay on my back and then made me promise to bring him home safe and sound before morning."

"Where did you lose him?" asked Titch, keen to

help the lion.

"As soon as we got to the woods, Shrimp leapt up into the trees and disappeared. He could be anywhere by now, but being a tree monkey I think he will still be somewhere in the woods. As you can see I didn't get back home last night because I've been looking everywhere for him. I simply can't face his mother. She will be very upset and very angry with me."

"Won't you be missed?" asked Titch.

"Not today, it's a rest day in the circus and my friend Horace will roar and pretend that there are two of us in the cage. But tomorrow, there's a show in the afternoon and if I am not back by morning, there'll be trouble."

"Oh dear," said Wiffen. "I don't think the human people will like the idea of a lion roaming around the countryside."

"I know," said Edgar. "They will have search parties out, with guns and policemen everywhere."

Wiffen jumped up quite alarmed. "We don't want search parties in our woods, especially with guns. It's all right for little pixies with magic bicycles, but where does a plump turkey hide?"

"You can bounce around in your magic boots," suggested Mitch, helpfully.

He received a withering look from Wiffen. "I can't bounce around the woods for ever. No, no, no, we can't have search parties in our woods. Absolutely not! We must find that monkey." He moved over to the fireplace and screeched up the chimney. "Budgie, come down here straight away."

A few moments later Budgie appeared at the other window and, looking sideways at Edgar, asked, "What's the matter?"

"We have to find a monkey called Shrimp. Would

you please speak with all the birds you can find and get them to fly over the woods and look as hard as they can?"

"All right," said Budgie, and immediately she flew off to see what she could find.

The presence of Edgar the lion had caused all the rabbits to hide in their warrens, but when Titch, Mitch, Wiffen and Perry came running out shouting for help, they all popped out into the open and gathered round.

Titch called to them all. "We need help. This is a friendly lion called Edgar, so there is no need to be afraid. There is a little monkey lost in the woods and we need to find him. Can you all go and look for him straight away and come back here when you have found him."

Immediately all the rabbits and other woodland creatures raced into the woods to go and search for Shrimp the monkey.

Titch turned to Edgar and said, "If that little monkey is in the woods, then someone will find him."

"I do hope so, for all our sakes," said Edgar, and then found himself a nice spot of shade to lie in.

It wasn't long before a hare came bounding out of the woods in great excitement. At the same time a

big, black crow landed beside them, cawing loudly.

"I've seen that monkey," said the crow. "It's on the little Blackberry Island."

"I can take you there," said the hare panting as it pulled up along side them. "I've seen him as well. There is a pond in the woods and in the middle of it there is a small island that's only big enough for one thing to grow and that's a blackberry bush."

"I've been there," said Perry. "There are some delicious blackberries growing on it and because there are not many creatures can swim over to the island there are always plenty of blackberries to be eaten."

Edgar was surprised and said, "Shrimp hates water. He could never swim over to the island. His mother has enough trouble trying to get him to wash his face, let alone take a swim."

The hare replied, "There are some trees that have branches overhanging the blackberry bush. It would be easy for a lightweight monkey to climb along a branch and drop down on to the island."

They all rushed into the woods and followed the hare and Perry until they came to a clearing and there they found a small pond with a small island in the middle of it. Sitting forlornly by the blackberry bush was a tiny monkey with his head in his hands and his tail hanging limp.

Edgar stood at the water's edge and roared over at Shrimp. "You are a naughty monkey! Where have you been?"

At the sound of Edgar's voice, the monkey jumped up and his tail started waving frantically.

"I was just exploring and then I couldn't find you anywhere," he cried, shrugging his little shoulders

and speaking in a shrill voice. "I just got lost."

"What are you doing on that island?" said Edgar, who turned to Titch and Mitch and added, "It's no use shouting at him, I'm just glad to have found him."

Shrimp shouted back and pointed to a branch dangling above him. "I climbed along that branch and jumped down on to this island. Then the branch swung back into the air and when I had finished eating blackberries, I found it was too high for me to get back into the tree, so I'm stuck here. I'm sorry Edgar. I really am."

The little monkey looked very sad.

"Jump into the water and swim over to us," called out Mitch.

"I'm too frightened," replied Shrimp. "I can't swim."

"It's very easy," persisted Mitch. "You just wave your arms like this." The pixie proceeded to thrash about on the ground with arms and legs waving everywhere.

"I'll drown," wailed the monkey.

It was no use trying to persuade Shrimp to swim. Even when two otters turned up and promised to help him across the water, he would not move.

Titch and Mitch had just decided to build a raft to float on the water, when all of a sudden Wiffen burst out of the bushes behind them. He was wearing his magic boots and striding along quickly. "Leave it to me," he called out as he passed the astonished group.

Without stopping, the turkey walked with big, long steps out onto the surface of the water and over to the island.

"Hurrah," called out the two pixies.

"Well done, Wiffen," added Titch, "You are clever. I'd forgotten that your magic boots can walk on water." They all watched as Wiffen arranged Shrimp on his back so that the monkey's arms were round his neck and he was sitting with his legs astride the turkey's back.

"Let's go!" they heard

Wiffen call out. Then the turkey simply walked on top of the water until he got to the bank in front of them and then let the monkey slide down to the ground.

"Thank you very much, Wiffen," said Edgar in a very relieved voice. "Now I can get back to the circus and nobody will ever know that we escaped."

"Yes, thank you, Wiffen," said Shrimp.

"I wish we could come and see your circus," said Mitch. "We've never seen tigers, elephants or performing horses."

"Or clowns and acrobats," added Titch.

Budgie landed beside them and said, "I know some birds that have perched on the big tent and peeped in through a hole in the top of it. You could take your magic bicycle right up to the top of the tent and do the same."

Titch turned to Edgar and asked. "Do you think we could?"

"Well," said the lion thoughtfully. "There is a big tent pole that goes right up to the top of the tent and there is a hole up there to let some air into the tent. So I suppose you could come and see the circus tomorrow."

"Brilliant," shouted Mitch. "Hurrah, we're going to the circus."

They all stayed with Wiffen and Perry in their little cottage until the middle of the night. Then, when it was very dark, Edgar set off for the circus. Shrimp, who had promised he would not run away again, rode on Edgar's back and clutched at the lion's mane to make sure he didn't fall off.

"We'll watch out for you tomorrow afternoon at the circus," called out Shrimp as he disappeared into the woods.

The next day, after taking lunch with Wiffen and Perry, the two pixies jumped on to their bicycle and called out the magic words, "Up, up and away!" At once, the bicycle hovered in the air. They flew higher and higher until they were over the woods and could see the town in the distance. Before long the big tent of the circus came into view and sure enough, there was a pole sticking out of the top of it. As they came down to land on the flat top of the pole they saw hundreds of children all walking towards the circus entrance.

To make sure their bicycle didn't fall off the pole, they tied it down tightly then wriggled in through the hole in the top of the tent. Just inside there was a small platform around the pole. It was just the right size for them to sit comfortably and watch the performance on the ground below them.

When all the children and their parents were sitting in their seats, a big band started to play some loud music and a parade of clowns and acrobats raced and tumbled into the circus ring. Immediately a mighty roar went up from the children who all clapped, laughed and cheered at the same time. They made such a loud noise that Titch and Mitch nearly

fell off their platform with surprise. They hadn't expected the children to be so noisy. But children can be very noisy indeed, and so they were, all the way through the afternoon. The two pixies enjoyed

watching the circus performers and the animals.
When Edgar the lion came on and walked around
the ring, roaring at the children, the two pixies
laughed and cheered him. Then, Edgar sat on a big
stool and roared again. As he did, he leaned back
and waved a paw at the top of the big tent. Titch and
Mitch knew he was waving to them and they cheered
themselves hoarse as they waved back.

3

The Hospital Tree

WIFFEN, THE MOST INTELLIGENT TURKEY IN
the world, was on a mission of mercy. He had
received a plea from Misty the fairy to deliver a
satchel of medicines to the hospital tree. The wings
of a fairy are very delicate and Misty was too
frightened to make the short journey over the sea to
the island, where a hollow tree was used as a hospital
for sick birds. The island was also the place where
Titch and Mitch lived.

It was quite early in the morning when Misty and
three of her friends had landed at the little cottage
where Wiffen lived with Perry.

"Good morning, Wiffen. Good morning, Perry."

Misty sounded very cheerful. "We've brought you some home made strawberry jam and we would like you to do something very kind for us."

Although Wiffen could be quite grumpy, especially early in the morning, he was very fond of Misty and was always very polite to her. "Of course Misty, we'd be delighted to help you. What would like us to do?"

"Just you, Wiffen. Unfortunately, Perry can't walk on water and that is necessary for the mission of mercy that we need you to undertake," said Misty, and she went on to explain the mission in full.

"And where would I find this hospital tree?" asked

Wiffen grandly, suddenly feeling quite important.

"It's over on the pixie's island," responded Misty. "So I would like you to walk over to the island, and go and see Titch and Mitch. They will know how to find the hospital; it's in a

hollow tree on top of a hill. All the sick birds go there for help."

Misty put a large cardboard box, filled with bottles of potions, tubes of ointments and little cartons of pills, onto the table and said, "These are all made by the fairies to help the sick birds in the tree. You need to find Nena, the barn owl; she's very clever indeed and heals all the sick birds who find their way to the

61

hospital tree. I know there's a very sick song thrush that needs an operation as soon as possible."

"I didn't know there was a hospital for sick birds on the island," said Wiffen. "Owls don't have hands or fingers. How can Nena mend birds?"

"Because the very skilful surgeon is Tambo the squirrel. Nena tells him what to do and she stands over him while he operates. There's a whole team of doctor and nurse squirrels working for Nena. They're all very

highly trained."

"Well, fancy that!" Wiffen was very impressed by this news. "I'd better get moving right away," he said, reaching for his boots.

The fairies sealed the box, then slipped it into the satchel, padded with scrunched up paper to protect it on the journey, and fastened it onto the turkey's back. Wiffen slipped his feet into his magic boots and they automatically gripped his claws firmly.

"Off I go then," he called out, and with a wave to Perry and the fairies, he left the cottage. Taking big

strides, he set off through the woods towards the coast and the sea.

It wasn't long before he reached the beach and, without a pause, carried on walking onto the waves. About half way to the island, he came across two men and a boy sitting in a small boat with fishing rods stretched out over the sea. As there was nowhere for Wiffen to hide, he just carried on walking across the water and right past the boat. The two fishermen had their backs to him but the boy stared in astonishment at the strange sight before him. As he passed the boat, Wiffen gave the boy a friendly wave and gobbled a greeting. The boy waved

back, mouth wide open in surprise, and blinked a few times. He seemed about to say something to the men about what he had seen, but thought better of it and went back to his fishing in silence.

Even with magic boots on, Wiffen's legs were aching when he arrived at the island and scrambled over the rocks to get to dry land. Unfortunately, he had never explored rock pools and did not know how very slippery they can be when covered with seaweed. Tottering on the edge of a particularly deep pool, his boots slipped, and he only prevented himself from falling in by flapping his wings madly. The satchel however slipped off his back and splashed into the water. Sprawled on a rock, Wiffen watched helplessly as the packet of important medicines slid slowly down under the surface and into the seaweed.

"Oh my word, oh my word," he muttered to himself and, taking off his boots, he used his claws to clamber down to the edge of the pool. He stared at the water to see if he could locate the satchel at the bottom, but the pool was too deep. All he could see was his own reflection, staring back at him. Shifting his weight slightly, he bent down to get closer to the water and peered even harder into its murky depths.

Suddenly, a large pincer came out of the water and grabbed his beak. With an enormous squeal, the

surprised turkey leapt backwards, pulling a large
lobster out of the pool as he went. It hung on to the
turkey's nose for just a moment before letting go and
falling back into the pool.

Wiffen scrambled back up the rock so fast that
his claws slipped on the seaweed and he slid down

into the rock pool with a great splash.

Squawking and flapping in the water, the frightened turkey tried to get back onto the rocks. Despite his best efforts, he kept slipping back down. Suddenly the lobster pinched his bottom so hard that Wiffen gave a shriek and flapped his wings so quickly that he actually flew out of the pool.

Landing with a bump, Wiffen was in a state of

shock. He danced all over the rock gobbling, squawking, and flapping. "Oh my goodness!" he cried. "What a terrible thing to do to a turkey! What an awful, horrid creature that lobster is! And how am I going to get the medicine back?"

For a long time, he prowled round and round the pool trying to work out his best plan of attack. At one point he shouted at the lobster. "Give me my medicine back. If you don't, I'll jump into the pool and then you'll be sorry." It was however an idle threat because, brave as he was, Wiffen did not intend to get close to that rock pool again. He sat down to think again, and then he noticed that blood was dripping from the end of his beak.

"I'm wounded," he said to himself. "I must get Titch and Mitch, they'll know what to do."

The two pixies where enormously surprised to see

Wiffen appear at their little house. He was soaked through, utterly bedraggled, and so angry he found it difficult to speak properly. "Mission of mercy - medicine – Nena the owl," he gasped and spluttered.

"Are you all right, Wiffen?" asked Mitch, full of concern. "Your beak looks very swollen."

"I know my beak is swollen and it's bleeding. It was grabbed by a giant lobster, a mean, vicious creature, that lives in a rock pool down by the sea." Wiffen was still in a furious rage.

"Why did the lobster grab you?"

Wiffen squawked incoherently again and his wattle turned a very bright red.

Titch produced a cup of tea and said, "Perhaps you'd better calm down, drink this tea and tell us what happened."

Eventually the irate turkey managed to tell the story of his mission of mercy and about the hollow tree for sick birds.

"I don't know where this tree could be," said Titch, scratching his head and trying to think.

"I do!" exclaimed Mitch. "I heard Budgie the seagull talking about a big barn owl who has set up home in the hollow tree on top of the hill. It's very near the plum tree and surrounded by a great thicket of thorn trees. You know, Titch, right where we get those delicious plums."

"Of course, we haven't been there for ages," said his brother.

"Oh good, now we know where it is," said Wiffen. "But how do we recover the satchel of medicine from the rock pool?"

"My goodness," shouted Mitch. "The tide is coming in. We don't have very long. We must do something soon or the medicine will be carried out to sea."

Titch made a decision. "We need to tell Nena the owl, so I'll fly the magic bicycle up to the hollow tree and you two go back to the rock pool and try to persuade the lobster to give the medicine back to Wiffen. If he doesn't like turkeys, he might like Mitch and give the satchel back."

So the friends separated and before long, Titch hovered over the hospital tree and looked down. It was a very big, old tree and there was a large hole in the side, which was right at the very top. There were also smaller holes dotted all round the trunk and a little door had been cut into the base of the tree. He called out, "Nena, Nena, are you there?"

From out of the big hole at the top of the tree, the head of a large barn owl appeared. It looked round, blinked in the bewildered way that owls do and said,

"Who wants me?"

"My name is Titch. I'm a pixie and I'm on an important mission. It's about your medicines!"

Titch landed the bicycle at the bottom of the tree and Nena flew down to join him.

After Titch had told his story, the owl walked around in circles thinking hard and then said, "A bad-tempered lobster, you say? Stolen my

medicines? We can't
have that. Let's go
and see this crabby
monster. I think I
may have an idea."

When Titch and
Nena landed beside
the rock pool,
Wiffen had already
worked himself into
another rage and
was calling the lobster all the most horrid names he
could think of, but all to no avail. The lobster stayed
under the water and never showed himself.

"I know you are in there," screeched Wiffen.
"Come on out you nasty, little bonehead!"

"Quiet down, please Wiffen," pleaded Titch, and
he led the fuming turkey away from the rock pool.
"Nena is here and she has an idea, so please be quiet
for a little while."

Nena whispered to the two pixies. "I'm going to
make the lobster jump out of the water and chase
me. When he does, you two have to leap into the
water, dive down and rescue the satchel of
medicines."

"All right," responded the pixies, "We'll be ready.

How are you going to get the lobster out of the pool?"

Nena blinked a couple of times. "Just watch and be very patient."

Then the barn owl settled herself at the edge of the pool, just out of reach of the pincer that had grabbed Wiffen's beak and, leaning over, she stared down at the water. For a long time she just stared and stared with her large yellow eyes and never moved at all. Eventually, the lobster found it all very unnerving, because he popped out his head, glared at Nena, and shouted out in a very rude way, "Who are you staring at, you great pop-eyed monster. If you want that satchel, you are not having it. It's mine now, so you can all go away." With that, the lobster ducked back down under the water and dropped to the bottom of the pool.

The owl never moved a muscle and she just kept staring at the water. After a while, the lobster popped its head out again and snarled at Nena. "Go away, it's bad enough having a great ugly turkey gobbling and raging at me without you just staring. I don't like it! Go away!"

This time Nena spoke very calmly to the lobster. "I have decided to drain all the water out of your pool and let all the birds come and peck at you."

The lobster sneered. "You can't do that! This rock pool has been here for ever and never lost its water. That's why I live here. It cannot be drained."

"Oh yes it can. There is a plug underneath this rock and I know where it is. When I pull it out, all the water will rush away into the sand and you'll be left stranded. I'm going to take it out right now."

Nena suddenly jumped off the rock and disappeared. The lobster leapt out of the pool shouting, "Oh no you won't! Just you wait until my pincer catches up with you! Come back here you horrid bird!" The lobster scrabbled over the rock and raced off on its clattering legs, chasing after the owl.

As soon as he left, Titch and Mitch, who had been crouching quietly on the other side of the pool, slid into the water. Taking deep breaths, they swam down to the bottom of the pool and grabbed the satchel. Holding it between them, they returned to the surface where Wiffen was waiting.

"Thank goodness for that!" he cried joyfully and, taking hold of the satchel in his beak, jumped off the rock and scuttled away across the sand. Meanwhile, the brave pixies scrambled out of the water and looked around for the lobster. He hadn't gone very far, and was standing on the sand glaring at Nena, who stood a little further away, staring back at him.

On an impulse, the lobster turned around and saw the pixies standing on the rock, dripping water everywhere. Realizing he had been tricked, he lurched around and, waving his giant pincers in front of him, chased after the pixies. But he was too slow. Titch and Mitch could run a lot faster than the

lobster and Wiffen, who was racing across the sand in front of them, was a long way away. So, with a cry of rage, the lobster stopped chasing them and instead trudged slowly back to his rock pool. When he reached it, he slithered back into the dark water and was gone.

When they were sure that the bad tempered lobster was safely back in his pool, the three friends looked for Nena. They found her standing on a large rock and looking up into the sky.

"What is it Nena? What are you looking at?" asked Titch and Mitch, craning their necks to look up.

They saw a bird with large wings and a long tail

flying in a straight line towards the hill behind them. As it got nearer, they noticed that it was carrying something in its claws.

"That's a heron," said Nena. "And herons never fly that fast. I believe there is something wrong, especially as it's flying straight to the hospital tree. I have to go. Be sure to bring the medicines up to the tree and I'll meet you there." Nena launched herself into the air and, in an instant, she was beating her

wings rapidly and flying straight back to the hospital tree.

Titch and Mitch jumped on to their magic bicycle and shouted out the magic words, "Up, up and away!" Within moments, they were flying towards the hospital tree and following Nena.

The heron had just landed on the ground when Nena reached the tree with Titch and Mitch following close behind.

"Tambo," shouted Nena. "Come quickly, I need your help."

A red squirrel came rushing out of the doorway of the tree. "What's the matter?" he said in a squeaky voice.

The heron was completely out of breath and gasped in reply, "It's my baby chick. She fell out of the nest and broke her wing. Please help her."

"Of course we will, right away," said Nena.

"We have no bandages left," said Tambo holding his hands out in despair.

"Some just arrived. They are in a satchel sent by Misty."

Tambo looked around.

"Where is the satchel?"

"Come on Titch and Mitch," said Nena. "Where is the medicine?"

The two pixies looked at each other, put their hands over their mouths and Titch said in a small voice. "We left the satchel with Wiffen."

Nena sounded quite cross when she said, "Then where is Wiffen?"

Everyone searched about them, but before they could speak, there was a great rustling behind the thorn hedge that surrounded the tree.

"Here I am!" A voice came from above them and,

looking up, they saw Wiffen wearing his magic boots and leaping high over the hedge.

"Well done, Wiffen!" they cried.

"It's a pleasure," said Wiffen as he landed with a great thump on the ground. "I have completed my mission of mercy."

"Thank you, Wiffen," said Nena. "You're quite a hero, and when I've seen to this chick, I'll be sure to come and bandage your beak."

"Thank you," replied Wiffen, settling himself down. "I'll be more than happy to wait. I believe somebody said something about a cup of tea?"

4

The Big Cheese

WIFFEN, THE INTELLIGENT TURKEY, WAS IN
a bit of a pickle. He admitted it to Titch and Mitch as
soon as the two pixies joined him in the living room
of his little cottage. Titch and Mitch were sitting
down, but Wiffen was prowling up and down with a
very worried expression on his face and seemed to be
having difficulties in explaining his problem.

"Ahem," he said, and cleared his throat with a
nervous cough. "You see, we were having tea with
Misty the fairy... she pops in from time to time you
know, just to see how Perry and I are getting on..."
He broke off, looked thoughtful for a moment, then
ruffled all his feathers, turned round and began to

pace up and down again.

Titch and Mitch looked at each other and smiled. They knew that Wiffen was very fond of Misty and would do anything for her. "What is the problem?" asked Titch.

"He was bragging again," interrupted Perry. The Old English sheepdog was lying on the floor in a corner of the room casually licking one of his paws. He spoke in a deep, rumbling voice. "He always shows off when Misty visits us. He can't help it."

Wiffen stopped pacing and glared at Perry with his bright little eyes flashing angrily. "I most certainly was

not bragging! I am, after all, the most intelligent turkey in the world, and Misty expects me to know lots of things."

"You don't know how to make cheese though, do you?" Perry raised his head and sniggered in a doggy sort of way.

"Perhaps not," admitted Wiffen. "But I'm thinking about it." He turned to the two pixies and continued. "You see, Misty came to tea yesterday. We had scones with strawberry jam and crackers with chestnut paste. Misty said how she thought the chestnut paste looked just like cheese and she was disappointed to discover it wasn't; it turns out that she loves cheese, but doesn't get to eat it very often because nobody she knows makes cheese."

"So," interrupted Perry again, "the big, silly bird said he would make some for her by next week."

"And so I will!" Wiffen shouted, shaking a wing at Perry.

After a bit more pacing about he turned to Titch and Mitch and spoke in a very quiet and calm voice. "Do you know how to make cheese?"

The two friends shook their heads.

"I'm afraid we don't know," said Mitch. "But we like cheese as well, so we'd love to find out."

"Let's make some then," said Titch. "I have an

idea," and turning to Mitch, he added, "Do you
remember when we met Cedric the Hermit? We were
looking for a pot of gold at the end of the rainbow
and he lived in a cave behind a waterfall."

"Of course," replied Mitch, clapping his hands.
"He had a great big book of knowledge! There's sure
to be a recipe for making cheese in it."

"Yes," shrieked Wiffen. "That's it. You two can go
to the hermit. Bring back the recipe and I'll make the
cheese."

"But it's a long way," complained Titch. "It will
take us the rest of the day to get there and back."

"Well you had better start off now," said Wiffen,
adding, as an incentive, "Just think how much you
like cheese. You can have half of all the cheese I

make.
I promise you."

When Titch and Mitch looked doubtful, Wiffen added another incentive for them to consider. "You know it's for Misty, and she really is a very lovely fairy."

"Oh, all right," said Titch.

"We'd better get going then," said Mitch nodding in agreement, "but, I believe we should make the cheese on the island. If it gets difficult, we have friends there who can help us."

Wiffen agreed and said he would use his magic boots and cross over to the island at first light. As they left the cottage, Wiffen implored them once more. "Please get the best recipe you can find. This cheese must be special, you understand?"

They nodded, and soon their bicycle was rising in the air and heading for the distant hills and the waterfall where Cedric lived.

About an hour or so later, they arrived at the waterfall that guarded the entrance to the hermit's cave. Leaving the bicycle parked safely under a Mulberry tree, they dashed through the cascading water and got themselves soaking wet. Then, ducking down to crawl along a narrow passage, they arrived in the candlelit cavern, and there, on the huge oak table, sat the great book of knowledge. But Cedric was nowhere to be seen.

"Cedric," they called out, but there was no reply.

"He must be out," said Titch, folding his arms and staring glumly around the cave. "What shall we do?"

Mitch looked at the book thoughtfully. "Cedric did say that we could look at the book any time we wanted, so long as we didn't actually take it anywhere. So why don't we just have a look?"

Titch agreed and together they stood on a chair and opened the book at the very first page. Reading down the list of contents, they looked for any subject that might be cheese related. They found nothing, so turned to the second page, then the third and the

fourth and so on. On page ten, the list of contents ended and they were beginning to lose hope when suddenly Titch gave a triumphant shout. "Here it is! On the very last page – How to make cheese."

The two friends took out a pen and paper and carefully wrote down every word of the recipe. Then they closed the book and Titch wrote a short note to

Cedric, so the hermit would know that the pixies had come to visit in order to consult the book of knowledge. They then returned to the magic bicycle and rode straight home for a well-earned rest.

The following morning they jumped out of bed nice and early, eager to make a start on their cheese making adventure. After a good breakfast, they studied the recipe and made a list of all the things they would need to make the cheese.

Just as they finished, the front door opened and Wiffen squeezed into their room.

"Good morning," he said cheerfully. "Did you get the recipe?"

Before the pixies could reply there was a knock on the front door. Wiffen opened it and, much to his surprise, found Percy

Hedgehog outside, standing on his back legs and sniffing the air hopefully.

"Mr Wiffen," he said at last. "Can I have some cheese please? I haven't eaten any cheese in a long time and I do so like it." Then he gave Wiffen a most beseeching look and smiled as nicely as he could.

"I haven't made any yet," said Wiffen in astonishment. "How on earth did you know I was thinking of making cheese?"

"Florence Squirrel said so, at the Hospital Tree!"

Wiffen spluttered. Percy continued.

"She's one of the nurses there, lives next door to me."

"Ah," said Wiffen, none the wiser.

"She heard it from Dora Dove."

"Dora Dove?" snapped Wiffen. "Who on earth..?"

"She went with Nena, the owl, to visit Misty about new medicines," said Percy Hedgehog, wiping his mouth with the back of a wet paw. "And apparently she overheard Misty tell Nena that Wiffen, the clever turkey, was making cheese for her."

A small grumble grew in Wiffen's throat. "I don't have any cheese so please go away," he said sharply, and shut the door in Percy's face.

He scowled at Titch and Mitch. "Now the whole world will know I'm making cheese," he complained.

"We'd better get on with it. What do we have to do?"

"We have the recipe," said Mitch, "allow me to read it out: Take a litre of fresh milk from a cow or a goat. In this case, it would have to be goat's milk because there are no cows on the island, but there are some wild goats living in the hills behind the woods."

Titch looked doubtful. "We don't know the goats very well, that might be difficult."

"Let me finish the recipe," said Mitch. "Add one teaspoonful of Rennet and shake it very vigorously for ages until lumps of yellow cheese can be seen."

"What's Rennet?" asked Wiffen.

"It appears," said Mitch, "that Rennet is a special ingredient that makes the cheese appear in the milk when it gets shaken."

"Where does this Rennet come from?" Wiffen asked impatiently.

"I was just about to tell you," said Mitch. "You have to make it. You take twenty stinging nettle leaves, chop them into tiny pieces, crush them and boil with water until the leaves go very soggy. Then you pour away the water and allow the nettles to dry out. This is Rennet and you use one teaspoonful for every litre of milk."

"Is that all!" cried Wiffen. "Then let's get started.

Who will get the stinging nettles?" He looked
straight at Titch

"Don't look at us," said Titch. "We are not going
anywhere near a stinging nettle."

"What about Percy Hedgehog," suggested Mitch.

"He'd do anything for some cheese and stinging nettles won't affect him. He might still be outside."

"Humph," said Wiffen. "I'll go and see."

When he opened the door he gave out a startled cry because crowding round the front door were all the pixie's woodland friends. As well as Percy Hedgehog, there was Big Jack Rabbit and Little Molly his daughter, Bertie Beaver and the little beavers from the stream in the woods. They had all arrived to meet Wiffen. Even Grumpy the Badger, who normally sleeps during the day, had made a big effort to visit the turkey. There were at least six squirrels and even more rabbits jumping up and down at the back of the crowd. The number of creatures who thought Wiffen had arrived to hand out cheese was quite astonishing.

The two pixies joined Wiffen in the garden and suddenly, Budgie the yellow seagull landed and pecked at Mitch's little green hat. "Come on," said the bird. "Where's all this cheese I've heard about?"

Wiffen shrugged his wings in despair. "It's that wretched hedgehog," he said. "He's told everybody he's met that I'm making cheese."

"Well, don't send them away just yet," said Titch. "You might need some help with this recipe."

The pixies returned to the house while Wiffen

talked to the crowd of animals.

A few minutes later, he joined them and announced. "Percy, Grumpy Badger and the squirrels have gone to find the nettles."

"Good," said Titch.

"Now, we need to shake up all this milk. Has anybody got any bottles?" added Wiffen, who was now well in control and starting to give orders to everybody.

"I know where there are lots of old plastic bottles," said Titch. "When Mitch and I go searching for things on the beach we find lots of bottles and we tidy them away in a little cave."

"Good. I'll get Big Jack Rabbit to go and get them."

Wiffen looked at Titch and Mitch thoughtfully. "You two can go and milk the goats. When the bottles arrive, you take Big Jack and the rabbits with you to help bring them back full of milk. Oh, and I think some more squirrels have arrived; you can have them as well."

Titch protested. "But Wiffen, we've never milked a goat before. We don't know what to do."

"The only thing you need to milk a goat is a pair of hands, and you two are the only ones here who have both the hands and the brains to do the job. I'd ask the squirrels but I can't see any goat with even a tiny bit of sense letting a squirrel get hold of her udders.

"What will you be doing?" asked Titch.

"I have to stay here and boil some water ready for the stinging nettles."

With a sigh of resignation, Titch and Mitch agreed to get the milk from the goats.

When Big Jack Rabbit returned, he had with him two old, plastic lemonade bottles in his mouth and the rabbits that went with him returned with one each, all of which added up to quite a few bottles.

"Well done," said Wiffen to Big Jack in a lordly manner. "Now will you please go with Titch and Mitch to milk the goats, and make sure you wash the bottles in the stream beforehand. We can't have dirty cheese now, can we?"

With sighs of resignation, the pixies led a procession of rabbits and squirrels up towards the stream. Once all the bottles were thoroughly washed, the procession carried on towards the meadow where the goats lived. They arrived a short while later to find seven goats standing in the field and munching happily on the long, fresh grass.

Clearing his throat, Mitch approached the nearest goat and said, in a very gentle voice, "Hello Mrs Goat, can we have some milk please?"

All the goats in the meadow stopped munching grass and turned their heads towards the pixies. They looked at them suspiciously, then at the bucket they were holding and the line of rabbits and squirrels standing behind them, each holding a lemonade bottle.

"Goodness, gracious me," said the nearest goat in a surprisingly high-pitched voice. "Two pixies and a lot of animals have come to drink my milk. I don't think so."

"Please, Mrs Goat," said Mitch as politely as he could. "It's needed to make cheese for Misty the fairy."

The goat turned away and called out shrilly, "Gertrude, would you look at this. Two pixies want to get milk from us."

Gertrude was a white and black spotted goat with a very whiskery chin. She sauntered over and laughed in a squeaky way. "Tee, hee, hee, they're a bit small. They won't be able to fill that bucket. They'll need it to stand on. Tee, hee hee."

"Wait a minute," said the first goat. "Maybe they can climb trees."

"Trees?" said Mitch, rather puzzled. "Of course we can climb trees, and so can the squirrels. But why?"

"Because," said Gertrude, nodding towards a far corner of the meadow, "there's a crab apple tree on the edge of the wood over there which is full of little apples that we can't reach." She licked her lips at the thought of them. "If you can collect some crab apples then you can have some of my milk."

"And mine," said the first goat.

"And mine," said another.

"Mine too," called out a big black goat that came galloping over.

In a matter of seconds the party found themselves surrounded by the goats, all talking and bleating in a very excited manner. More goats appeared from behind bushes and shrubs to join them. Soon, the noise of the gathered goats was almost deafening.

"ALL RIGHT!" shrieked Titch at the top of his voice. "You have a deal. We'll collect the apples for you."

When they arrived at the bottom of the tree, the two pixies were about to climb when a crab apple hit Titch on the head. "Yeoow," he called out. "Who did that?"

Looking up he saw the mischievous face of one of the squirrels peeping down at him. "Stand out of the way, Titch," he shouted. "We're going to have some fun."

The squirrels were true to their word. They had climbed the tree first and were now busily plucking every crab apple they could find. The little orange fruits started whizzing out of the tree in a veritable shower, most of them aimed at the pixies, the rabbits or the goats. There was a strange cacophony of sound as the goats laughed in high-pitched voices. The rabbits ducked and squealed and the pixies chuckled as they dodged the flying crab apples. The high-spirited squirrels moved quickly and in no time at all, they had stripped the tree of all its fruit.

When the friends had collected all the crab apples there was a huge pile ready for the goats to eat.

"All right pixies," said Gertrude. "Well done, warm up your hands and collect your milk."

The squirrels came down from the tree and helped the pixies to milk the goats. It was hard work but eventually all the bottles were full and they said thank you to the goats and started the journey home.

"Hurry up," shouted Wiffen, when they appeared at the cottage. "You've been ages. Grumpy has brought all the nettles we need, I have chopped them up, boiled them and now they have been dried out and are ready to use."

Wiffen was already lining up the bottles and

tipping a teaspoonful of the dried nettles he now referred to as Rennet into each bottle.

"There we go," he said triumphantly. "We've done it. Come on everybody; shake up the milk, just like it says in the recipe."

Everybody grabbed a bottle and tried to shake it. The rabbits had managed to drag or carry the milk back from the farm but the bottles were far too heavy to shake vigorously. The same went for Titch and Mitch and when Grumpy Badger tried, the bottles kept slipping out of his claws so he couldn't shake them either. Even Wiffen tried but soon had to give up because the bottles were just too heavy.

"Oh dear," he said glumly. "That's disappointing. What do we do now?"

For some time, everyone sat round wondering and thinking, but none of the creatures had any suggestions to make.

Budgie arrived and said, "I've been watching you lot from that tree over there. Why have you stopped working? Is the cheese ready?"

"The bottles are too heavy to shake," said Titch sadly.

"Well," said Budgie, after some thought. "If you took all the bottles to the top of the hill and rolled them all the way down to the bottom, then they would get very shaken up indeed."

All the creatures stared at Budgie, and then Wiffen let out a whoop. "Of course! Why didn't I think of that?"

"What a good idea," added Mitch. "There is an old sack at the back of the cottage. We've also got a rope, which we can tie to the sack and drag the bottles up the hill."

They filled the sack with the bottles of milk and tied the rope to it. Then all the woodland creatures grabbed hold of the rope and dragged it to the bottom of the hill.

"Now then," said Wiffen. "I will stay at the bottom of the hill to rescue the bottles as they arrive and all of you will climb the hill pulling on the rope. Hurry, hurry, we haven't got all day."

Grumpy was tied to the front of the rope with Big Jack Rabbit right behind him, then came the rest of the rabbits, the beavers, the hedgehogs, the water rats and the two pixies, while the squirrels pushed at the sack from behind.

They set off trudging slowly up the hill. Half way up they heard Wiffen call to them from the bottom. "Mind you take it as high as you can, the bottles need a good shaking."

When the animals reached the top of the hill they were quite out of breath. Titch untied the rope round Grumpy and they all let go. The sack of bottles went bouncing down the hillside. With a whoop and a cheer all the animals raced after it.

By a stroke of luck, the sack came to rest at Wiffen's feet. By the time the animals arrived and gathered round him he had removed several bottles and was examining them closely. "Ahem," he said. "Nothing to see yet. But these bottles need a lot of shaking so off you all go, back up the hill and roll the sack down the hill again."

The animals all groaned together. Titch said, "How many times do we have to do this? I'm tired already."

"Until I return," announced Wiffen. "I have things to do, so you need to roll the sack down the hill lots of times, if you want to make cheese. I'll be back later and no slacking while I'm away."

A reluctant procession took hold of the rope again and trudged wearily back up the hill, dragging the heavy sack behind them.

It was late in the afternoon when Wiffen woke from the snooze he was having in the shade of an old oak tree. He jumped up with a start, hurriedly brushed down his feathers, then rushed back to the bottom of the hill to see how the cheese making was getting on. He arrived in time to see the sack come rolling back down for what must have been the tenth time. It was beginning to look very battered and worn. Behind it came the crowd of animals all quite out of breath and evidently jolly exhausted.

"That's it," announced Mitch, flopping down in

the grass. "I've had enough. I just can't go back up that hill."

"Me neither," agreed Big Jack Rabbit, who was panting and shaking his head.

"I see cheese," announced Wiffen, as he examined a bottle from the sack. "Tiny specks of yellow cheese floating in the milk. Come on everybody, just one more big effort and we'll be there."

"It will have to be the last time," said Titch. "I'm worn out."

"It will be," agreed Wiffen "I promise."

So the procession marched slowly back up the hill. By the time they reached the top, the creatures were totally exhausted. When they recovered their breath, they gathered round the sack and, with a mighty heave, pushed it over the edge once more. As it began to tumble, a loud tearing sound split the air, the sack opened wide and all the bottles spilled out. Bouncing free of the torn sack, they span wildly down the slope, picking up speed as they went.

"Quick!" cried Titch. "Catch them or they might break!"

With startled cries, the animals raced off after the cascading bottles, doing their best to catch them before they burst.

However, the bottles went a lot faster than

anyone could run. They banged, bounced, spun and crashed their way towards Wiffen, only to arrive at the bottom of the hill at the same time and going very fast indeed.

Realizing he was standing in their path, Wiffen let

out a mighty shriek and turned to flee. However, he hadn't got very far before the bottles caught up with him. One bounced up high and banged him on the back of his head. "Yoiks!" he squealed. Immediately another landed on his back. "Yaroo," he yelped. Then all the bottles bounced into him or around him before finally they landed onto a pile of rocks and stones.

The turkey sank to the ground battered and bruised by the bottles and looked around him. The bottles had all burst when they hit the stones, but where the milk was draining into the ground it left behind shiny, yellow lumps of cheese.

In spite of all his bruises, Wiffen yelled out excitedly, "I've done it! I've made cheese! Look at it."

Before Wiffen could get to his feet, the animals arrived in a great rush. They spotted the cheese lying all over the rocks and, with a triumphant cheer, grabbed as much as they could and started to eat it as quickly as possible.

"It's delicious," shouted Grumpy the Badger.

"It's the nicest cheese I've ever tasted," called out Big Jack Rabbit.

"Yum, yum," spluttered the squirrels.

"Leave it alone," shouted Wiffen in anguish as he saw all his cheese disappearing. "STOP EATING MY CHEESE!"

But the animals didn't listen. The cheese was too good for them to stop eating it. When all the cheese was gone, the animals started to disperse, licking their lips and saying, "Thanks Wiffen, the cheese was ever so nice. Do make some more one day."

Finally, only Titch, Mitch, Budgie and Wiffen were left behind,

standing forlornly in amongst the rocks and staring at all the empty bottles with very sad looks on their faces. None of them had even got to taste the slightest morsel of cheese.

"It's all gone," wailed Wiffen. "I've worked my feathers off, I'm covered in bruises and all I've got to show for it is a pile of empty bottles and not a single slice of cheese. What am I going to tell Misty?"

"All is not lost," said Budgie, flapping her wings proudly. "As I flew down I noticed two bottles of your milk lying in the long grass just behind the stones. None of the animals noticed them so you still have some cheese, Wiffen, and you honour is saved!"

Wiffen jumped to his feet with renewed vigour. "What a relief," he cried. "Well done Budgie. Thank you! Thank you! We must take them back to my cottage to show Perry and prepare the cheese for Misty." Turning to Titch and Mitch, he added. "Come on you two, and you Budgie; we'll have a cheese party tonight."

The two bottles of milky cheese were duly rescued from the long grass and taken carefully over the sea and back to Wiffen's cottage, where an excited Perry greeted them.

"Well," he asked. "How did it go?"

"Just you wait and see," said Wiffen proudly, marching inside. Titch and Mitch followed, carrying the precious cargo in their arms.

Back inside, Wiffen opened up the bottles and

poured away the milk, leaving behind lumps of nice, soft cheese. Perry sniffed eagerly.

"Hmmm," he said. "Not bad."

"And now to share it out," said Wiffen.

Firstly, enough cheese was saved for Misty's tea and crackers, then the cheese that was left was piled

onto a plate and the five friends had a tasty meal of bread, cheese and hot, steaming tea as they told Perry the story of how the cheese was made.

But, when they had finished, Wiffen just had to have another grumble. "All those wretched animals ate my cheese," he muttered through a clenched beak.

"Actually Wiffen," said Titch, wiping the last few crumbs from his mouth. "You've made a lot of animals very happy with your idea of making cheese, and when you think about it, they actually did all the work."

"Absolutely," agreed Perry, speaking from the corner where he had settled himself once more. "And making the animals happy is something you can brag about."

5

Helping Father Chistmas

ONE MORNING, TITCH AND MITCH WOKE UP
to find it had snowed during the night. They opened
the front door and saw a crisp blanket of fresh, white
snow covering their garden, the woods and
everything else for as far as the eye could see.

"Let's build a snowman," shouted Mitch, rushing
into the garden. He was very excited, and as soon as
Titch walked out of the house, he threw a snowball
at him.

It was two days before Christmas and the two
friends were planning to have a big Christmas party
for all their friends on the island.

"This snow will make our party very special," said

Titch, as he gathered some snow together to make a snowball to throw back at Mitch. Mitch, however, was now staring up into the sky and pointing. "Look," he said. "There's an aeroplane coming towards us, flying very low."

Turning round, Titch saw a small plane coming towards them over the snow covered meadow. "It's going to land!" he cried.

The noise of the engine got louder and louder and with a screech of brakes the aeroplane landed on the snow and skidded towards their little house.

"Yaowww," called out Titch in fright. "It's going to crash!"

The plane turned sideways and skidded to a stop just beyond their garden gate.

The two pixies stood open mouthed with surprise as another pixie, just like themselves, stood up in the cockpit and

called out: "Hey there, are you Titch and Mitch?"

The newcomer jumped out of his plane and ran over to them. He was dressed in a great red jacket with matching red trousers and a tight red hat. He even had a red scarf tied around his neck and rosy red cheeks from the cold snow that blew about him.

"Come on boys, get the kettle on; I desperately need a cup

of tea." The newcomer took off his hat to reveal curly, red hair. "My name is Robin," he said. "But most people call me Red."

"I wonder why," said Titch with a smile, as the pixie marched past them and into their house.

He settled himself down on the sofa and looked around. "My, oh my! You do have a snug little home here."

"Who are you?" asked Mitch.

"I am Father Christmas' chief recruiter and I am here because he needs your help."

"What?" cried the pixies together. "Father Christmas wants our help!"

"He does indeed! This morning he flew off to the far east where Christmas day starts earlier than here, and before he went he said, 'Red Robin, we are falling behind in our plans. Get some more helpers. I want all the children's sacks packed with their presents before I return.' So I looked at my list of pixies and your names were right at the top. Will you come with me to help Father Christmas?"

The two friends looked at each other and shouted, "Yes, we will!"

"Hurrah," said Red Robin as he drained his cup of tea. "Come on, there's no time to waste. We must be on our way. But first you must wear as many clothes as you can because we're off to the North Pole and it is gong to be very cold on the journey."

After searching for every item of clothing they could find in their little house and pulling them all on, the two pixies climbed into the little plane, squashed themselves into the small seat behind Red Robin and snuggled down as low as they could. Red Robin pulled a pair of goggles over his eyes, slid the roof of the cockpit shut and, with a happy cry of 'Away we go', he started up the engine. When the propeller was up to speed, the aeroplane roared off over the snow-covered meadow. Pulling back on the joystick, Red took the plane soaring up into the sky and away towards the sea. Titch and Mitch were off to help Father Christmas.

Peering out of the window, Titch and Mitch saw they were flying very fast through thick, white clouds. They had lots of questions they wanted to ask Red Robin, but the plane made such a loud noise as it whizzed along they couldn't hear themselves speak.

Eventually, they felt the plane tilt gently downwards and soon they came out of the clouds and into the clear air. Below them, they could see mountains covered in snow and frozen rivers of ice. It looked very cold indeed.

"Look!" said Titch, and he pointed into the distance where a castle perched right on top of a rocky outcrop.

Red Robin flew his aeroplane straight toward the castle and, as they got nearer, they could see the castle was much bigger than either of them could have imagined. Finally, they flew over the castle walls where they saw a narrow runway laid out for the plane. Red Robin landed the plane with great skill and brought it to a stop. Before unfastening the cover he said, "I suggest you run as fast as you can to the door over there," and he pointed to a large green door in the side of the castle. "It's too cold to hang around. Off we go."

Pulling the roof of the cockpit back, Red Robin leapt out of his seat and, closely followed by the excited pixies, he raced towards the green door. As they ran, they found the air so cold it almost took their breath away. On reaching the door, it opened sharply by itself and they tumbled inside, falling onto a thick, green carpet. When they got their breath back, they stood up and looked around.

They found themselves standing in a vast hall with high, vaulted ceilings and sheer walls criss-crossed by wide galleries and stairways. Dotted along the galleries were hundreds of small doors of

all shapes and sizes. The doors opened and closed repeatedly with loud creaks and bangs that echoed throughout the hall. As they looked about, Titch and Mitch could see small figures running from door to door, either carrying large bundles in their arms or clipboards on which they were making notes.

The next thing they noticed was the huge stone fireplace on the other side of the hall. A glowing fire crackled in its grate and looked very welcoming indeed. Tearing off their heavy coats, they ran over to the fire and started to warm themselves up.

Just then, a teddy bear, dressed like a butler, reached out a white-gloved paw and said in a very efficient voice, "If you will give me your coats, young sirs, I will have them cleaned, dried and warmed ready for your departure."

"Thank you very much," they replied together and handed over their many jumpers and coats.

"Follow me," said Red Robin smartly. "We have work to do." And he set off at a brisk pace down a nearby corridor and into the depths of the castle. As they followed him, they came across lots of other pixies, and also elves, fairies and goblins, all rushing around as fast as they could carrying small sacks of presents or pushing little carts loaded with toys and other goodies.

"This is what I want you to do," explained Red Robin, handing Titch a thick bundle of letters he had just been given by a passing elf. "One of you reads out the lists the children have made while the other packs all the required toys into the sacks, so they can be delivered into childrens' bedrooms by Christmas morning. Once the sacks have been filled, you take them to the reindeer hall where other helpers will load them onto the correct delivery sledge. When Father Christmas comes back tomorrow night, every toy for every child will be in the correct sack on the correct sledge ready for delivery." He stopped and looked at Titch and Mitch, who were staring at the thick pile of letters.

"Simple, isn't it?" said Red Robin proudly, then he frowned a little. "It should all go like clockwork, except that we are a little behind at the moment."

They arrived at the centre of the castle, which was another great hall even bigger then the last, brightly lit with coloured lights and decorated with floating streamers and balloons. Corridors leading into it came from all over the castle.

Red Robin stopped by a small door and said, "This is where you work. What you do is..." He broke off and looked with very raised eyebrows at a small, chunky looking goblin who had appeared out of a nearby corridor closely followed by a procession of walking toys. The goblin was grinning from ear to ear, shaking his head from side to side and calling out in a singsong voice to the procession behind him:

"Marching toys, in a line,
Left, right, left, keep in time,
Onwards go, don't look back,

Follow me into the sack."

When he saw Red Robin glowering at him, his cheeky grin quickly vanished. He stopped marching and all the toys following him banged into each other and fell down.

"Glimp, you naughty goblin! What have you done?" roared Red Robin, his face glowing even

redder than before. "Those toys should not be live toys."

The goblin looked very sheepish.

"You've been using a magic spell to bring the toys to life. THAT IS NOT ALLOWED!" Red Robin roared. His face looked as if about to burst.

Glimp looked anxiously all around him and, taking off his little pointed hat, held it in front of him and stammered, "If you please, Mr Robin, I was trying to help by making all the toys walk to the packing room and climb into the sacks. It's much quicker that way."

"Where did you get the spell?" asked Robin, calming himself down a little.

"I read about it in the Pinocchio book. The good fairy made a little wooden puppet come alive with a magic spell, so I sneaked into Father Christmas's study and found it on a piece of paper stuck to the wall." Glimp the goblin looked quite pleased with himself for a moment.

Red Robin spoke again, this time in an icy, cold voice. "And how many rooms did you enter and how many times did you use the spell?"

Glimp wasn't good at numbers, so he just held up all his fingers, looked at them and said, "That many, I think."

Red Robin covered his head in his hands and moaned.

Titch and Mitch looked at each other in astonishment, wondering what the problem was. It seemed quite a good idea for the toys to pack themselves into sacks. It would certainly save time.

Suddenly, out of one of the corridors came an icy blast of cold air and a short figure covered from head to toe in icicles rushed towards them, his cries getting clearer with every step. "Take cover! The toys are out!" He was waving his arms and shouting as he ran, leaving trails of broken ice behind him.

As he passed, he waved an icy hand at the two pixies, sprinkling them with cold, shimmering flakes of ice, then he raced on through the hall and disappeared down another corridor.

"Who's that?" asked Mitch.

"Jack Frost," replied Red Robin, looking extremely concerned, "And from the looks of him, I'd say he wasn't very happy."

Red Robin looked at the pixies. "Oh dear," he said, with a heavy sigh. "Oh dear, oh dear, what am I going to tell Mr C.?"

Titch was about to ask who Mr C was, when out of the corridors came a torrent of toys, running and jumping over each other like an avalanche. First

came a fire engine, with its sirens screeching and
bells clanging and firemen hanging off every side.
This was closely followed by a spaceship, piloted by a
very rugged looking pilot. Behind them came bears,
dolls, puppets, soldiers, robots, dinosaurs and all sorts

of strange and wonderful contraptions, many of which Titch and Mitch had never seen before.

The noise of the approaching toys got louder and louder as they all arrived with a rush. A little bear, dressed in a red scarf, and his friends, were all crammed into a toy railway engine. They were going far too fast and Titch and Mitch had to jump out of the way or be run over. With a great clatter of shouting, crying, cheering, laughing, booing and clapping, the great hall filled up very quickly with toys that had come to life.

Titch and Mitch, along with Robin, squashed themselves into a corner of the room and watched in stunned terror as the toys raced around, thoroughly enjoying themselves. Some were very naughty indeed; a toy dinosaur was taking itself very seriously by standing in a corner and roaring as loud as it could. It kept sweeping

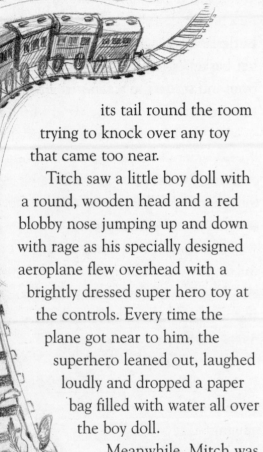

its tail round the room trying to knock over any toy that came too near.

Titch saw a little boy doll with a round, wooden head and a red blobby nose jumping up and down with rage as his specially designed aeroplane flew overhead with a brightly dressed super hero toy at the controls. Every time the plane got near to him, the superhero leaned out, laughed loudly and dropped a paper bag filled with water all over the boy doll.

Meanwhile, Mitch was watching a circle of puppet toys dressed in blue and white pyjamas holding

132

hands, jumping up and down and shouting, "Hurrah for Father Christmas." Next to them were a large number of identical teddy bears having a picnic with Little Red Riding Hood, but as soon as she opened her basket of food, a great pack of fluffy dogs rushed over and started to scrap with each other for the tastiest portions.

As they stood staring, a green railway engine gave a loud screech on its whistle and roared towards the pixies again. In the cabin stood a slimy yellow space alien with a wild look on his face and no obvious intention to stop. Titch and Mitch leapt out of the way just in time and the space alien crashed his train into a pile of building bricks with a joyful yell.

Robin shook his head sadly. "This was bound to happen," he said, wiping his brow with a red hanky. "When toys come alive they need to be taught how to behave. They don't know that live creatures can be hurt by being knocked down."

A crowd of toys were gathered round one door singing:

"Nellie the elephant packed her trunk
And said goodbye to the circus,
Off she went with trumpety trump,
Trump, trump, trump."

As if on cue, an enormous rubber elephant came charging into the room and the toys all cheered. Unfortunately, the elephant was too big for the doorway so it crashed through the doorframe which splintered into pieces. The elephant, unaware of the damage, let out a great trumpeting noise and all the toys cheered again.

A group of identical little girl dolls had found a dolls house and brought it into the great hall. Unfortunately, they set it down too near to the toy dinosaur, who promptly knocked down the chimney pot with a sweep of its tail. The dolls burst into tears, which prompted a group of builders to rush over waving hammers, screwdrivers and ladders. They all tried to put the chimney pot back but couldn't decide which one of them would actually do it, so they started fighting amongst themselves. This made the little girl dolls cry even louder and eventually all the builders fell on top of the dolls house and it broke into pieces.

Another very naughty doll with a white face and long plaits had opened tins of face paint and showed great skill by grabbing passing toys and smearing their faces with a variety of colours. A very surprised puppet doll had been given the face of a spider and a toy nurse doll had the whiskers and eyes of a lion

painted on her face. However, when she tried to turn
fairy queen toys into zebras by painting them black
and white they objected so strongly that all the cans
of paint were spilled and a great morass of black,
yellow, white, green and red paint slopped all over
the floor. After that every toy that passed by slipped
on the paint and became covered in the gloopy,
colourful mess.

It was no use Robin or the pixies trying to restore
order; there was so much noise, the toys couldn't
hear a word they said.

"Whatever can we do?" wailed Robin.

"How about another magic spell?" suggested
Mitch. "There must be a spell to turn them back into
normal toys."

"Of course there is," agreed Robin. "But how
could we ever make them hear it?"

"Maybe Father Christmas could stop them,"
shouted Titch, as they rushed out of the great hall.

"No, no, no, he's not back until tomorrow, and by
then it'll be too late!" roared Robin. "We have to get
them back NOW! Follow me!"

The three of them went straight to Father
Christmas's study and began to search. The room was
large, with a big, ancient wooden desk standing in
front of an enormous window. On pieces of paper

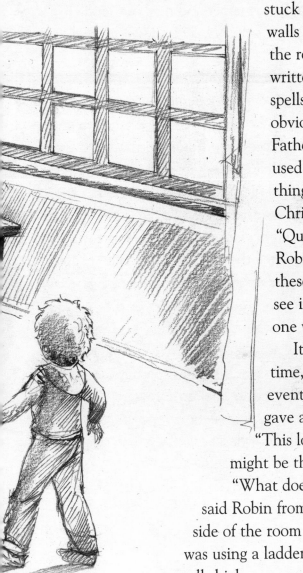

stuck on to the walls all round the room were written many spells. It was obvious that Father Christmas used magic to get things done at Christmas time. "Quickly," said Robin. "Read all these spells and see if we can find one we want."

It took some time, but eventually Titch gave a cry of joy. "This looks like it might be the one!"

"What does it say?" said Robin from the other side of the room where he was using a ladder to read the spells high up near the ceiling.

Titch held up the paper and read out loudly:

"Sprinkle Magic Dust No. 5 high in the air and say the following words:

Sprinkle on girls and sprinkle on boys,

Turn all the presents back into toys."

"Well done!" said Red Robin as he raced over to the big desk and started to rummage though the drawers. "Ah-ha! Here it is!" he said, triumphantly holding up a small glass jar. "This is Magic Dust No. 5! Back to the great hall boys."

They all raced back down the corridors towards the main hall. Once they reached the balcony, Red Robin held up the jar and called out the magic words. He was about to tip the jar over the troublesome toys when he realized to his horror that no one had heard a single word. He tried again.

"Sprinkle on girls and sprinkle on boys,

Turn all the presents back into toys."

Again, there was no reaction.

"Just pour the powder!" cried Mitch.

Red shook his head sadly.

"It's no use. They have to be listening, otherwise it falls on deaf ears."

He hung his head sadly and looked as if about to weep.

But then, in amongst the crowd of unruly

playthings, Titch saw something quite extraordinary.

"Look!" he pointed. "Look down there!"

The others looked to where he pointed. Down in the middle of the hall, surrounded by chaos, stood a toy; a live toy, but a toy with a difference, for this toy was trying to keep order.

"It's PC Plod!" cried Red Robin, triumphantly.

"And he needs our help," added Titch and darted off back towards the study.

"Where's he going?" Red Robin asked Mitch.

The little pixie could only shake his head. "I have absolutely no idea," he said.

It was not long before Titch came running back waving his arms gleefully.

"I've got it!" he cried. "Enlarging powder! Just like Father Bong used."

"Huh?" Red Robin was baffled.

"That's right!" cried Mitch. "Enlarge PC Plod!"

Red Robin scratched his head. "I don't understand."

"Watch," said Titch. "And be amazed!"

Running down a flight of stairs, with Mitch close behind him, Titch stormed into the middle of the seething mass of insane toys. As he reached PC Plod, he flung a handful of bright green powder over the poor policeman. Suddenly, and very much to his surprise, PC plod began to enlarge. As he grew bigger and bigger, the other toys around him started to notice and stepped back in fear at the huge figure of authority before them.

Finally, he reached his full height and, in a great booming voice, shouted "Everyone, stop! This is the police!"

Like a blanket of fresh snow, silence fell over the whole room. Titch looked up at Red Robin, still standing on the balcony with the jar of Magic Dust No. 5 in his hands.

"Now!" he hissed, "Sprinkle it now!"

As Titch and Mitch ran for cover, Red Robin scattered the contents of his little jar and called out the magic words once again. This time everyone was listening, and within seconds the hall, which had been filled to bursting with wayward, disorderly toys, became a hall full of normal playthings.

Red Robin breathed a huge sigh of relief. Out of corridors and passageways, elves and gnomes and pixies, who had all been hiding from the chaos, crept out and began to tidy away the toys into boxes and sacks and cart them off to the Reindeer Hall, ready for departure. In a few short moments, normality had returned to the castle and the real job of sorting presents for Christmas got underway once more.

"Well," said Red Robin, turning with relief to his two helpers. "I have to say that without you I don't know what we'd have done. Thank you so much."

"We are just glad to help Father Christmas," said Titch.

Mitch pulled the bundle of children's letters from his pocket. "I believe we have a big job to do and very little time left in which to do it."

"Of course," shouted Robin. "I must get the helpers working as fast as they can." Then, turning to the pixies, he added, "And thanks to you two, the children will still all have a happy Christmas!"